D0410269

# Disney PRINCESS

# 5 Minute Treasury

## PaRragon

Bath · New York · Cologne · Melbourne · Delhi
Hong Kong · Shenzhen · Singapore · Amsterdam

This edition published by Parragon Books Ltd in 2015

Parragon Books Ltd
Chartist House
15–17 Trim Street
Bath BA1 1HA, UK
www.parragon.com

Copyright © 2015 Disney Enterprises, Inc.

All rights reserved. No part of this publication may be reproduced, stored in a retrieval system or transmitted, in any form or by any means, electronic, mechanical, photocopying, recording or otherwise, without the prior permission of the copyright holder.

ISBN 978-1-4748-2529-0

Printed in China

# Contents

The next morning, the princess showed her coat to Suzy, one of her mouse friends. "Isn't the Prince thoughtful?" Cinderella remarked.

"Nice-a! Nice-a!" Suzy exclaimed. The coat sleeve felt warm and cosy – especially compared to where the mice lived.

A few minutes later, Jaq and Gus went into Cinderella's room. It had been a chilly night in the attic, and the mice were still shivering.

"Cinderelly! Cinderelly!" Jaq called. He knew that if he told the princess how cold the attic was, she would do something about it. But she was rushing off to get dressed for a tea party, so she didn't hear her friend.

3

Jaq sighed. It was too cold for the mice to stay in the attic much longer. Cinderella had always been very kind to the mice, and Jaq was sure she would want them to be warm.

So he and Gus called the rest of the mice down from the attic. They sat in front of a blazing fire in Cinderella's room. Before long, their cold paws and tails had warmed up, and their teeth stopped chattering. They'd wait there until Cinderella got back.

Soon, the new housekeeper came in to clean the room.
When she saw the mice, she shrieked and shooed them away.
"Mice don't belong in the castle!" she yelled. "Now get out!"

The housekeeper didn't know that the mice were
Cinderella's friends. She chased them with a broom.
The frightened mice had no choice but to scramble
back up to the cold attic.

"Brrrr." Gus began to shiver as soon as the mice were safely upstairs.

The mice really needed the princess's help! But how would they be able to speak to Cinderella when they were afraid to set foot downstairs?

WHAM! Suddenly, the castle gardener barged through the attic door. Before the mice knew what was happening, he had trapped them.

"Now take them outside!" they heard the housekeeper say. "Take them far away so they never return!"

Cinderella was right. The gardener had been trying to make a decision. He was about to let the mice go as the housekeeper had ordered. But he was worried about them. He knew it was too cold outside.

Finally, he decided to take the mice to the stables. "Now don't tell the housekeeper," he told the stable workers. "But these poor mice need a warm place to stay and a bite to eat."

The mice were very grateful to their new friends.

The mice nestled together in the barn. But as night approached, the stables got colder. Luckily, the horses were very friendly. They told the mice to snuggle in their manes to keep warm.

"Thassa nice-a," said Gus as he drifted off to sleep.

Later that night, back at the castle, Cinderella was starting to worry. She hadn't seen the mice since that morning. Jaq and Gus nearly always came by in the evening.

Cinderella was searching for the mice when she ran into the Prince.

"Why, hello!" the Prince said. "Are you looking for the same person I am?"

"No, I don't think so," Cinderella replied. "I'm looking for the mice!"

"Ah," said the Prince. "Well, I am looking for our new housekeeper. Apparently she threw the mice out of the castle today!"

"Oh, no!" Cinderella cried. "Poor dears. They'll freeze outside!"

"Don't worry," the Prince said. "The mice have found a new friend." He told Cinderella about what the gardener had done.

Together, Cinderella and the Prince went to the stables. They thanked the gardener and the stable workers. Then they gently woke the mice.

"Cinderelly! Cinderelly!" the mice shouted happily.

Cinderella was relieved to see her little friends safe and sound. Though the stables had been nice, the mice were glad to return to the castle.

From then on, Cinderella made sure the mice always had a warm place of their own – in one of the main rooms of the castle.

The crab raised his baton, and the musicians began to play. Beautiful music filled the sea, until – *CLANG*!

"Who did that?" Sebastian demanded.

"Um ... I did," a young mermaid named Coral replied quietly.

"The best way to play the cymbals is to hold on to them! Now, if there are no more interruptions," Sebastian said grumpily, "let's continue."

The rehearsal went from bad to worse. Coral dropped her cymbal a second time. *CLANG!* Then she stumbled and landed on top of a kettledrum.

As Ariel watched, Sebastian threw down his baton. "Rehearsal is over!" the crab yelled and stormed off.

Ariel helped Coral up. "Don't mind Sebastian," she said.

"I'll never be able to get this song right – let alone perfect!"
Coral said sadly.

"Don't worry about it," Ariel said. "The only thing *I'm* perfect
at is making Sebastian mad. You should have seen his face the last
time I went to the surface."

"You've been to the surface?" Coral asked, amazed.
"You must be the bravest mermaid ever!"

"It's just something I like to do," Ariel said. "I'm always
gathering treasures. Would you like to see my collection?"

"I'd love to!" Coral exclaimed.

The two mermaids swam to Ariel's grotto.

"Make yourself at home," Ariel told Coral when they arrived. Flounder the fish was there. He waved a fin at them.

The young mermaid swam around, examining jewellery and shiny trinkets. "Where did you find all of this?" Coral asked as she put on a strand of pearls.

"I found some of it in sunken ships," replied Ariel.

"You've been inside a sunken ship?" Coral said with a gasp. "Weren't you scared?"

"Of course not. Were you, Flounder?" Ariel teased.

"Nothing to it!" the fish fibbed.

"So what are we waiting for?" Ariel asked. "Let's go!"

Coral and Flounder trailed behind Ariel. Soon they arrived at a ship that had sunk to the ocean floor.

"Let's see what's in there!" Ariel urged.

Her friends followed her through a large porthole.

Inside the ship, Ariel found an old steamer trunk. "Look at this!" she cried, holding up a purple parasol.

"And this!" Coral exclaimed, picking up a fancy lampshade. "I wonder what it's for?"

"My friend Scuttle can tell us," Ariel said. "Follow me!"

"Where are we going?" Coral asked Flounder.

"To the surface," he replied matter-of-factly.

Soon the friends arrived at the surface. Scuttle the seagull examined their treasures. "That is a *twirleriffer*!" he said, looking at Coral's lampshade. "It's what human ladies wear when they're going somewhere important."

Before long, the friends had to leave. As they headed home, Coral asked Ariel if she could keep the *twirleriffer* at the grotto. "It might get broken at home," she explained.

"Of course," Ariel agreed. "The grotto is my secret place, and it can be yours, too."

A few days later, as Ariel swam towards the grotto, she heard someone singing. The voice was strong and clear – but sweet, too.

When Ariel arrived, she saw her new friend.

"Coral! I didn't know you had such a lovely voice! You should be singing in the concert, not playing the cymbals."

The little blonde mermaid shrugged. "I just like singing to myself," she explained. "I've never actually performed."

The next day at rehearsal, Sebastian made Ariel and the orchestra
practise over and over, but something always seemed to go wrong.

"The big day is tomorrow!" the crab said, fretting.
"This concert needs to be fit for a king – King Triton, to be exact!
Let's try it again." So they did. The rehearsal went on and on.

By the end of the afternoon, everyone was tired. "See you
tomorrow," Ariel said. Her voice was raspy.

On the day of the concert, Ariel could only whisper. She had lost her voice! Luckily, she knew who could take her place.

"Me?" Coral said when the princess asked her. "But I can't!"

"You must!" Sebastian insisted. "Otherwise King Triton's birthday celebration will be ruined!"

"I can't sing in front of a crowd of merpeople," Coral said.

"Sure you can," Flounder said.

Coral thought about how she had visited a sunken ship and gone to the surface, things she had never thought she could do – all because of Ariel. Now her new friend was counting on her.

"All right," Coral said slowly. "I'll do it."

That night, when Coral peeked out from backstage, she nearly fainted. The entire kingdom was there – including her parents and her brothers and sisters! King Triton and Ariel sat in the royal box.

When it was time, Coral took a deep breath and swam onstage. As the orchestra started playing, she sang softly. But as she went on, Coral's voice got louder. Before she knew it, the concert was over, and the audience began to clap and cheer.

"Coral," said Sebastian, smiling, "you can give away your cymbals. From now on, you're going to be a court singer!"

After the show, Ariel went to congratulate her friend. She found Coral with her family.

"I didn't know you could sing like that!" one of Coral's sisters exclaimed.

"No one ever would have known if it wasn't for Ariel," replied Coral. "She believed in me."

Ariel still couldn't speak, but she gave Coral a big hug. It had been a wonderful evening.

# Beauty and the Beast
## Belle and the Castle Puppy

Belle was strolling through the castle garden one chilly spring day when she heard a whimpering sound. A puppy was huddled outside the castle gates. He looked cold and dirty.

"Oh, you poor thing!" Belle cried. "Let's get you warmed up and fed!"

She wrapped the puppy in her red cloak and hurried to the castle.

Belle and the enchanted objects gave the puppy a bath.
The coat stand brought a towel.

When he was clean and dry, the puppy ate a bowl of
warm stew.

"He's so cute! I hope we can keep him!" Chip the
teacup exclaimed.

A moment later, the foot stool ran past Belle and the others. His legs were muddy.

"The foot stool dug up the garden!" Belle exclaimed.

"But why?" asked Lumiere the candelabrum.

As Belle watched the foot stool chase after the Beast, she suddenly understood.

"Oh, poor little guy," she said. "He just wanted some attention, too!"

Suddenly, the puppy raced after the foot stool, barking playfully. They both disappeared among the trees.

"What if they don't catch up with the Beast? They'll get lost!" Belle exclaimed. "I have to bring them back safely."

"But it's getting dark," Mrs Potts protested.

Belle looked at the long shadows creeping through the forest. Clutching her cloak tightly, she took a deep breath and headed for the trees.

"Wait!" Lumiere called to Belle. "I'll come and light your way."

"Thank you," Belle said as she picked up the candelabrum. "I'm glad you're coming."

"Me, too. I think," Lumiere replied. But his flames flickered nervously.

Belle walked along a path. She had come this way before.

"Puppy! Foot stool!" she called.

She hoped that they had met up with the Beast. She was looking forward to returning to the castle.

A moment later, something rustled in the bushes.

"What is that?" Lumiere whispered.

"I hope it's just squirrels," Belle answered.

"They must be very big squirrels," Lumiere replied.

Belle picked up a large stick. Then she and Lumiere walked on, calling for the puppy and the foot stool.

Belle realized that the puppy and foot stool
had got lost. She was determined to find them.

A short while later, Belle heard loud barking.

"I think we've found them!" Lumiere exclaimed.

Belle followed the sound until she came into a
clearing. The foot stool and puppy stood under
an enormous tree. The puppy was growling
and barking loudly.

"What's wrong?" Belle wondered aloud. Then she looked round and gasped. Two large wolves were nearby.

"The puppy is protecting the foot stool!" Lumiere exclaimed.

"He's too small to stop those wolves for long," Belle said. "He needs help!"

Quickly, Belle put Lumiere on the ground and lit the stick she had been carrying. She ran towards the wolves, swinging the stick.

"Get away! Get away!" she shouted.

But the wolves didn't move.

Just then, the Beast showed up. The wolves ran away, yelping with fear.

"The puppy tried to save the foot stool!" Belle told the Beast.

"They are brave little fellows," the Beast answered.

Cradling the puppy in one arm and the foot stool in the other, he led Belle back to the castle.

Later that night, everyone settled by the fireplace.
Belle watched the Beast stroke the foot stool and feed
biscuits to the puppy.

"May the puppy stay until I can find him a home?"
she asked.

The Beast cleared his throat. "His home is here – with us,"
he answered gruffly.

Belle smiled. She was glad that the Beast had changed
his mind.

The very next day, the Beast presented the puppy and the foot stool with shiny badges. From now on, they would be the official protectors of the castle.

*Yip! Yip! Woof! Woof!* They couldn't have been more excited.

# THE PRINCESS AND THE FROG

# A Surprise Guest

It was a balmy afternoon in New Orleans – perfect for a night with friends.

"Charlotte, honey!" Big Daddy LaBouff called to his daughter. "How about going to Tiana's Palace for supper tonight?"

"Oh, Daddy, that would be wonderful! Just give me a minute to change."

A little later, Big Daddy and Charlotte drove off. But they didn't realize their dog, Stella, was asleep in the back of the car!

When the LaBouffs arrived at the restaurant, a jazz band was on stage. Louis the alligator was playing his trumpet.

"Charlotte! How are you?" Princess Tiana exclaimed. She was happy to see her best friend. "Big Daddy, would you like to sit with my mama and Naveen's parents?"

"Why, I can't think of anyone better to share my supper with than Eudora and your in-laws," he replied.

Soon Tiana's family and friends were settled at a big table. The princess walked around the dining room to make sure her other guests were happy, too.

Late that night, after the last jazz number had been played, all of the guests went home. Charlotte and Big Daddy never realized that Stella was also at the restaurant! "Ta-ta!" Charlotte called as they left.

Eudora left with Naveen's parents. Turning to her daughter, she said, "I have never heard the band play quite that well. And that new gumbo – absolutely delicious. I'll see you tomorrow, sweetheart."

After Princess Tiana walked her family to the door, she went back to the dining room to finish cleaning up.

A few minutes later, Louis and the band went to the kitchen for their evening meal.

As they walked in, Stella began to bark. *Grrr! Woof!* She was terrified of the giant alligator.

"Oh, now hold on, little dog!" Louis said to Stella. "I'm not here to eat you. I just wanted a taste of the chef's new gumbo!"

But Stella was frightened. She kept barking.
The kitchen staff and the band members looked at
each other. They weren't sure what to do.

In the dining room, Tiana and Naveen heard the barking. They rushed to see what was causing the commotion.

Tiana recognized the LaBouffs' pet at once. "Stella? What are you doing here?" she asked. "Don't worry. Louis is our friend. He wouldn't hurt anybody."

"That's true!" Naveen cried, putting his arm round Louis. "He is nothing but a big guy with an even bigger heart."

The alligator peeked out from behind his tail. He didn't understand why the dog was so upset.

Stella looked at him suspiciously.

"Go ahead," Princess Tiana encouraged the dog. "Just go over and make friends."

Cautiously, Stella walked towards Louis. The alligator stayed very still. He didn't want to frighten the dog all over again.

"See? Nothing to be scared about!" Naveen said.

Soon Stella realized Louis was harmless. The dog wagged her tail. Then she smelled some delicious chicken.

Tiana smiled. "Let's get dinner for you all."

The princess and the kitchen staff quickly put together a supper out of that evening's leftovers.

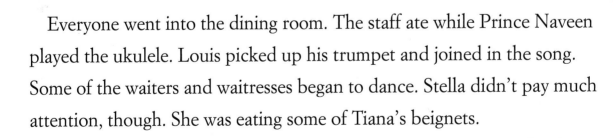

Everyone went into the dining room. The staff ate while Prince Naveen played the ukulele. Louis picked up his trumpet and joined in the song. Some of the waiters and waitresses began to dance. Stella didn't pay much attention, though. She was eating some of Tiana's beignets.

A while later, the staff headed home. Tomorrow would be another busy day at Tiana's Palace.

"Come along, Stella," Tiana told the dog. "Time for you to go, too."

The prince and princess took Stella to Charlotte's house. No one had noticed she was missing yet!

"Goodnight, Stella," Princess Tiana said, giving the dog a big hug. "Now that you know how much fun we have at the restaurant, you should come by more often."

*Woof! Woof!* Stella barked. She hadn't expected to have such an adventure that night. She knew she'd return to Tiana's Palace the next chance she got.

# Aladdin
## The Desert Race

Jasmine and Aladdin were strolling around the palace grounds
one evening when the Sultan ran out on to the balcony.

"Drat!" the Sultan cried. "Oh, drat, drat, drat – that dratted
Desert Race!"

Jasmine was surprised. Usually her father loved the Desert
Race! Every year, the best riders from Agrabah competed against
those of the neighbouring kingdom of Zagrabah. The fastest
horse and rider were awarded the prized Golden Palm trophy.

"What's the matter, Father?" Jasmine asked.

The Sultan shook his head sadly. "I just heard that Prince Fayiz will be riding for Zagrabah again. His horse is so fast he's won the race the last three years in a row!"

"I have an idea, Father!" Jasmine said eagerly. "I could ride Midnight in the Desert Race this year. He's the fastest horse in Agrabah!"

"Oh, dear me, no!" The Sultan looked shocked at the very suggestion. "The Desert Race can be dangerous. I won't have my daughter risking her neck like that!"

Aladdin spoke up. "How about if *I* ride Midnight in the race?"

The Sultan's face brightened immediately. "What a splendid idea!" he cried. "You'll have such fun, my boy!"

The day of the race arrived. Riders from Zagrabah paraded into Agrabah. Prince Fayiz rode in on his impressive white stallion, Desert Warrior.

"I don't know why we bothered to bring the Golden Palm trophy," Fayiz announced haughtily. "We'll only have to carry it back to Zagrabah later."

Fans from both kingdoms gathered to watch the race. Soon the riders took their places at the start line.

The Sultan looked at Aladdin. "What an odd-looking horse that boy is riding. I wonder why I've never seen it before." But he didn't have time to worry about that.

"Now, where is Jasmine?" he wondered. "It's time to start the race!" But the princess was nowhere to be found.

"We can't wait any longer, I suppose." The Sultan raised a flag to signal the start of the race. "One, two ... three! And they're off!"

The riders galloped into the desert.

A black horse with a mysterious veiled rider took the lead right away. As soon as they were out of view of the palace, the rider threw off the veil. It was Jasmine!

"I do hate going against Father's wishes," she whispered to Midnight. "But I just had to prove that you were the fastest."

Aladdin was curious about the rider on the black horse. "Jasmine!" he gasped when he saw her.

73

Just then, his horse spotted the cool, inviting water of an oasis.

"Now that's more like it!" exclaimed the horse. Except the horse was actually the Genie! He jumped into the water and took the shape of a sea horse.

"Hey! This wasn't part of the plan!" Aladdin cried.

"Don't worry, Al," the Genie said. "We'll catch up. Gotta stay hydrated, you know!"

On land, Jasmine and Midnight galloped off without a backwards glance.

Fayiz and Desert Warrior were starting to catch up. They were shocked when they saw the princess. Fayiz didn't want to lose to her.

Jasmine urged Midnight on, but the other horse was very fast. Finally, Desert Warrior pulled ahead.

"Give up now!" Fayiz shouted. "That trophy will always belong to Zagrabah!"

But Midnight wasn't finished yet. He surged forward again ... and passed Desert Warrior!

"Not so fast!" Jasmine called to Fayiz with a laugh. "That trophy is in Agrabah, and that's where it is going to stay!"

Fayiz and Warrior stayed on Midnight's heels ... until the horses had to jump a ditch that crossed the path. Midnight sailed over easily, but Warrior skidded to a stop!

With the other team out of the running, it seemed there was nothing to keep Jasmine and Midnight from winning. But then the princess heard the sound of hoofbeats close behind her.

"What?" she cried, looking back.

It was Aladdin! Jasmine hadn't even known he was still in the race!

Soon Aladdin and his mystery horse had caught up, and he and Jasmine were fighting for the lead. Jasmine was glad that the trophy would stay in Agrabah no matter which one of them won. But she *really* wanted to prove that Midnight was the fastest horse in the two kingdoms. She urged him on.

The two horses were neck and neck as they neared the finish line. First Midnight pulled ahead a tiny bit, then Aladdin's horse did. But neither could keep the lead....

And so, the two horses crossed the finish line at the same time.

As soon as Midnight slowed to a stop, Jasmine jumped off, gave her tired horse a hug, and led him to the water trough. Then she walked over to Aladdin.

"Congratulations!" he said.

"Same to you," Jasmine replied. "But where in the world did you find such a fast horse?"

"Er ..." Aladdin looked at his horse. Then he looked at his feet. "Um, that is ...." He didn't seem to know what to say.

"Surprise!" the Genie cried, transforming back into his usual form.

Jasmine gasped. "Genie? That was *you*?"

"Sorry, Princess Jasmine," the Genie said, winking. "We were just *horsing* around."

Aladdin grinned sheepishly. "It was my idea. I couldn't bear the thought of Zagrabah winning again this year."

Snow White knew the Dwarfs worked hard. That day,
she wanted to make sure that when they got home, they
didn't have to do any more work – no dusting, no sweeping
and no cooking.

Snow White waited until the Dwarfs had left. Then
she and her animal friends hurried into the cottage.

The princess looked around. "By the time the Dwarfs get
home tonight, our surprise will be ready."

So they set to work. Snow White sang a cheerful song as she
swept the cottage floor. The birds chirped while they picked
up crumbs. The squirrels used their fluffy tails to dust. And the
chipmunks and deer washed and dried the breakfast dishes.
With so many helpers, Snow White had the downstairs gleaming
in no time.

Next, they went upstairs, and the princess began to make the beds.

"Pull the covers up tight," she told the bunnies. "Then fold down the top. There, it's perfect!"

The bunnies hopped off to start on the other beds.

Before long, every inch of the Dwarfs' cottage was neat and tidy. Snow White and the animals headed outside to gather fresh berries, nuts and apples to use in the Dwarfs' supper.

"They'll be very hungry after their long day," said the princess. Luckily, the blueberry bushes had lots of ripe fruit, and the basket was quickly filled. "I know what we'll make for dessert," Snow White told the rabbits. "Blueberry pie!"

Next, the princess and her friends strolled into a meadow to find some wild flowers.

"Lovely!" said Snow White as she sniffed a blossom. "These will be perfect for the table."

Inside the cottage, Bashful had one more guess. Whoever was behind the surprise would have to be one tired Dwarf! And who seemed the sleepiest? Why, Sleepy, of course!

The truth was, Sleepy wasn't the only one. After a long workday, their tummies pleasantly full, all Seven Dwarfs were ready for bed.

When they climbed the stairs, the Dwarfs found one last treat: seven neatly made beds and seven perfectly fluffed pillows. As they drifted off to sleep, the Dwarfs decided to tell their good friend Snow White about this wonderful surprise the very next time they saw her.

# Sleeping Beauty

## Buttercup the Brave

"Which horse would you like to ride today?" a stable groom asked Princess Aurora one morning.

Aurora looked around the royal stable. There were so many horses! It was always hard to choose. But then a fine palomino caught Aurora's eye. He was the most beautiful creature she had ever seen!

The next day, Aurora decided to ride Buttercup out to the fairies' cottage.

"Why don't you let me saddle up Samson and come with you?" Phillip suggested, looking worried.

"Don't be silly," Aurora said with a laugh. "I grew up in those woods, remember? Besides, I'll be with Buttercup. He'll take care of me!"

Aurora and Buttercup pranced off. But the moment they entered the woods, Buttercup became a different horse.

He began to walk slowly and look around nervously. When some of Aurora's woodland friends appeared, Buttercup even tried to run away!

"What's the matter, Buttercup?" Aurora asked.
"Why, there's nothing to be frightened of!"
    She could hardly believe the change in her horse.
He was even afraid to step over a branch.
    When she asked him to walk through a forest
stream, he nearly fainted!

By the time she reached the cottage, Aurora was feeling a bit frustrated. How could a horse who was so brave at the palace be so timid in the woods?

Flora, Fauna and Merryweather hurried out of their cottage.

"Oh, what a beautiful pony!" Merryweather exclaimed.

Aurora sighed. "He *is* beautiful," she said. "But he seems to be afraid of everything in the woods!"

"I'm sure it will be all right," Flora said. "You'll just need to be patient with him, that's all."

Aurora watched her new horse change colour. That didn't seem to bother him at all. But when a stray leaf fluttered down, he jumped and snorted as if it were a horse-eating dragon.

What was she going to do? She didn't want to give up on him. Buttercup was so perfect in every other way.

Soon it was time to say goodbye to the fairies. Aurora did her best to ignore the way Buttercup hesitated at every shadow on the way home. She had been certain that Buttercup was the perfect horse for her. Now she wasn't so sure.

Suddenly, Buttercup stopped abruptly.

"What is it *this* time?" Aurora asked with a sigh.

Then she looked at the path ahead ... and gasped in horror. An enormous mountain lion was blocking their path!

Aurora's heart pounded as she watched the creature creep closer. If Buttercup could be scared by a bunny rabbit, he was certain to go crazy over a mountain lion.

They were in big trouble!

To Aurora's surprise, Buttercup didn't panic or try to run. Instead, he stood proudly and puffed himself up to look even bigger and snorted angrily at the mountain lion.

Then he marched forward and struck out at the lion with his front hooves! Aurora hung on. She was still scared. But it seemed that Buttercup wasn't!

Aurora stroked Buttercup's neck and talked to him in a soft voice, reminding him to stay calm. The butterfly fluttered closer and closer ... and finally landed right on his nose (which was only trembling a *little*).

"Good boy!" she said, praising him. "You know, Buttercup, I think we make a perfect team!"

# Beauty and the Beast

# A Friend for Phillipe

It was a beautiful morning when Belle arrived at Phillipe's stable with a surprise for her friend. "Guess what I have!" she called happily as she hurried to the horse's stall. "The first carrots of the season, Phillipe! I picked them just for you."

Phillipe was not as happy as Belle had hoped. He sniffed at the bunch of carrots. But when Belle offered him one, the horse pushed her hand away.

"Is something wrong?" Belle asked, alarmed. Phillipe was always hungry.

Phillipe hung his head and sighed.

Belle decided that she had to cheer up her friend. But how?

"If only you could talk," Belle said, "you could tell me exactly what to do."

Later that morning, Belle hurried to the castle library. She gathered
all the books about horses she could find and began to read.

"*Sacré bleu!*" cried Lumiere when he, Cogsworth and Chip saw all
the books. "What are you doing, Princess?"

"I want to cheer up Phillipe," Belle explained. "I hoped these books
would help me figure out what's wrong, but I'm not having much luck."

"You should brighten his stall!" Lumiere suggested. "It's important
to have the right atmosphere, you know!"

"I believe that music is the key to happiness," Cogsworth said.
"It always made me smile when I was an enchanted clock."

"Or how about a bubble bath?" Chip chimed in. "That used to
cheer me up!"

Belle decided to give each idea a try.

First, she and Lumiere decorated Phillipe's stall. They covered the walls with wallpaper and sprinkled flower petals on the floor. They piled cushions in the corners, hung curtains on the windows and strung up beaded garlands. For a final touch, they hung a chandelier from the ceiling.

"*Voilà!*" Lumiere exclaimed. "What more could
a horse ask for?"

Phillipe stared sadly out of the window.

"I wish I knew," said Belle.

Next, Cogsworth brought an orchestra to the stable.
Belle, Lumiere and Chip listened politely as Cogsworth led
the musicians through a very long concert.

Phillipe didn't seem to enjoy the music, though.

"Welcome to our castle!" Belle told the new horse when they arrived. "We're honoured to have you as our guest!"

To show the horse she meant it, Belle fixed up the stall next to Phillipe's.

"There," she said when she was done. "Now this looks like a stable where a horse – or two – could live happily ever after!"

And that is exactly what they did.

# Cinderella

## A Royal Friend

"The princess is coming!" a crowd of girls exclaimed as they watched Cinderella's coach approach their school.

"Let me see!" cried Emma, who had arrived at the school only a few days earlier. "I want to see the princess!"

"Don't worry, you will," replied Claire, who was the oldest. "She's coming to visit us."

Sure enough, the coach came to a stop right outside.

A royal trumpeter blew his horn loudly to announce Cinderella's arrival.

"Quickly, girls, gather round," said the headmistress. She hurried to open the door. "Welcome, Your Highness!" she exclaimed. She and the girls curtsied as Cinderella entered the room.

"It's so nice to see you all again," said the princess.

Cinderella liked to stop by the school to help the girls with their reading and writing.

She also brought books, clothes, toys and food. Many of the girls were poor and had few things of their own. Everyone was happy to see Cinderella. But no one was more excited than Emma.

Cinderella and the girls spent a wonderful afternoon together.

After their lessons, they sang, danced and told stories. Then they read together and played with some of the toys the princess had brought.

When it was time for Cinderella to go, she made an announcement. "In one week, there will be a party at the castle – to be held in your honour."

"For us?" the girls shouted excitedly.

"But what will we wear?" asked Emma.

Cinderella smiled. "Why, the dresses I am having made for each of you, of course! And you shall have new shoes and gloves as well! I remember how much fun it was when I got to dress up for a ball the first time. I thought all of you would like to wear fancy gowns, too."

Cinderella thought the seamstresses had brought Emma. The princess remembered what it was like to do chores all day. So she invited Emma to have tea with her.

They sat at a table laid with delicate china and gleaming silver. A servant brought in tea and cakes and biscuits.

"It must be wonderful to be a princess," Emma said between bites. "You get to wear fancy clothes, go to parties all day, and order servants around."

Cinderella laughed. "When a princess wants something, she asks politely. And there's much more to being a princess than clothes and parties," she replied. "Why don't you help me this afternoon and see what a princess *really* does?"

For the next few hours, Emma and Cinderella put together baskets of food, clothing, books and toys. Emma's favourite part was going through Cinderella's wardrobe to look for old clothes that could be donated.

Soon, it was time to deliver the baskets to the schools and orphanages. As they passed through the village in the royal carriage, Emma waved at a passer-by. *Princess Emma*, she thought. *I like the sound of that!*

When they arrived at her school, the headmistress gave
Emma a big hug. "Where have you been?" she cried.
"We've been so worried."

The headmistress and the other girls had been looking
for Emma all afternoon.

"But I thought the seamstresses brought you to work,"
Cinderella said, puzzled.

Emma explained how she'd sneaked into the castle.
"I'm sorry," she said. "I didn't mean to make anyone
worry. I just wanted to see what being a princess was like."

"Being a princess is more than just playing dress-up,"
Cinderella told her. "It also means being responsible."

"Why don't you come to the castle each day?" Cinderella suggested. "Then you can learn more about what princesses really do."

Every afternoon when Emma's lessons were over, she went to the castle. The princess was always very busy. She oversaw the castle staff. She visited the shopkeepers and farmers to make sure everything was running smoothly. She even got the court jester to tell jokes to children who were ill.

Emma tagged along everywhere. Cinderella decided she should help plan the party for the girls' school.

So Emma helped to decorate. She also helped the cook make a cake.

Cinderella was so impressed that she asked her mouse friends to make a special dress for Emma.

"It's fit for a princess!" Emma exclaimed when she saw it.

Finally, the night of the party arrived. The girls twirled around the dance floor in magnificent new dresses.

"I still wish I could be a real princess," said Emma.

"Because you've worked so hard, I'm going to make you an honorary princess for the evening," Cinderella said with a smile.

"Oh, thank you!" the girl cried happily. She was thrilled that she'd get to be Princess Emma for one magical night.

# Tangled

## Rapunzel's Story

Once upon a time, there was a magical kingdom ruled by a good queen and a kind king. They were happy until the queen became very sick.

The King had heard of a flower with healing powers and sent his guards to dig it up. Unfortunately, the flower belonged to a wicked woman named Mother Gothel.

But Rapunzel had a bargaining chip – the crown.
She'd return it only if Flynn helped her.

So Flynn reluctantly climbed down the tower, and
Rapunzel used her hair to lower herself to the ground.

The outside world was like a dream come true to her.
She'd never run through grass before, or climbed a tree,
or sat in a field of flowers. Still, she felt nervous.
Mother Gothel had said the outside world was scary.
And Mother Gothel wouldn't lie ... would she?

Flynn tried to frighten Rapunzel into going home. He took
her to the scariest place he knew – the Snuggly Duckling. It was
a tavern full of thugs!

The thugs glared at Rapunzel, but when she sang about her
dream of seeing the lanterns, they all became friends. The men
even showed Rapunzel and Flynn a secret passage out of the
tavern ... just in time, too. The palace guards had tracked down
Flynn and his stolen crown.

As they were escaping, Flynn hurt his hand on a sharp rock. That night, Rapunzel wrapped her hair round it, and his hand was healed!

Flynn was amazed, so Rapunzel explained about her magical hair. "But once it's cut," she said, "it loses its power."

They sat close together by the campfire. Flynn was starting to fall for Rapunzel. And Rapunzel liked Flynn a lot, too. But could she trust him?

Meanwhile, Mother Gothel had discovered that Rapunzel was gone. She began to search for her.

The next morning was Rapunzel's birthday. Flynn led her to town, which was just as wonderful as the woods. She and Flynn danced and ate cake, and then they took a boat to watch the lanterns.

"For the best day of your life, I figure you should have a decent seat," Flynn said.

Twilight came, and glowing lanterns filled the sky. Rapunzel was so excited to see the lights that she almost tipped the boat over.

"I have something for you, too," she told Flynn. She handed him the crown. She finally trusted him.

Flynn knew what he had to do.

Flynn went ashore and tried to give the crown to the Stabbington brothers – but the thieves knocked him out. Then they found Rapunzel and convinced her that Flynn had turned her in.

"A fair trade," they said. "A crown for the girl with the magic hair."

"No!" Rapunzel cried. She tried to run away, but she couldn't.

*THUMP! CRASH!* Mother Gothel rushed in. She rescued Rapunzel from the thieves. But she didn't tell Rapunzel she'd told the brothers to capture her in the first place.

Mother Gothel and Rapunzel returned to the tower. But Rapunzel couldn't stop thinking of everything she'd seen. Suddenly, all the pieces fell into place. "I'm the lost princess," she realized.

Mother Gothel froze.

"It was you!" Rapunzel said bitterly. "I should have been hiding from *you*."

Instantly, Mother Gothel stopped pretending to be nice and tied up Rapunzel. Soon Flynn came to the tower, looking for Rapunzel. Mother Gothel hurt him.

Rapunzel knew she could heal Flynn with her hair. "I'll stay with you," she promised Mother Gothel. "Just let me save him."

"Swear it," Mother Gothel said. And Rapunzel did.

Flynn refused to let Mother Gothel win. Grabbing a shard
from a broken mirror, he sliced off Rapunzel's hair. Immediately,
it turned brown.

"What have you done?" Mother Gothel shrieked. As
Rapunzel's hair lost its power, Mother Gothel became very, very
old. Soon she was gone.

Rapunzel held Flynn tight. Without her hair, she couldn't heal
him. He slipped away.

A single tear fell from her face. It landed on Flynn and began
to glow. His eyes opened. The magic in her tear had saved him!

Overjoyed, Rapunzel and Flynn went to the palace.

Rapunzel was welcomed by the king and queen, her real
mother and father. They couldn't have been happier to have their
daughter back. She wasn't the baby they'd lost any more, but she
was a lovely princess.

And although Rapunzel's hair was no longer magical, she was
still the most enchanting girl Flynn had ever met.

# Sleeping Beauty

## Aurora and the Helpful Dragon

"I'll race you to the lookout point!" Princess Aurora called to Prince Phillip as they galloped through the forest one sunny morning. She sped away on her horse, Buttercup, with Prince Phillip close behind.

As they rounded a bend, a small dragon popped out from behind a tree.

The prince and princess went to it at once.

Just then, Crackle noticed a kitten in a basket of wool. Crackle listened to it purring. Then he scrunched up his mouth and closed his eyes. He tried to purr. "*Purrgrr, purrgrr!*" Clouds of smoke streamed from his nose and mouth.

"Aachoo! Aachoo! Ah-ah-ah-CHOO!" The fairies sneezed so hard from the smoke that they tumbled backwards!

Crackle looked sad for a moment. Then he saw the kitten playing with a ball of wool, and he snatched some. *WHOOSH!* The wool burst into flames! Merryweather put out the fire with her wand.

"Oh, Crackle," Aurora said gently. "You're not a kitten. You're a dragon."

Crackle's lower lip trembled.

A moment later, Phillip led the horses into the stable. A dog followed, barking and wagging his tail. Crackle ran after them, wagging his tail, too.

He tried to bark. *"Woofgrr, woofgrr."* Flames shot from his mouth, and some straw caught fire.

Phillip poured water on the burning straw.

"You're not a dog," he said kindly, shooing Crackle away.

Sadly, the little dragon crept out of the stable.

Aurora noticed that Crackle looked unhappy, so she took him to the castle. As the princess began to tell a story, a bird sang by the window.

Crackle's ears perked up. He tried to sing like a bird.

"*LAAAlaagrr!*" he bellowed.

King Hubert heard the racket and rushed into the room.

"Oh, my, my, my! How did a dragon get in here?" he shouted.

Crackle had never heard a loud, angry voice before. Frightened, he ran to the garden.

Before Aurora could answer, thunder boomed and dark clouds covered the sky. As Aurora and Crackle ran back to the castle, rain began to pour down. Everyone was gathered in the grand hallway, watching the storm.

"I'm afraid King Stefan and the queen might lose their way," Prince Phillip said, concerned.

Aurora looked at Crackle. "Do you want to show everyone that you're a kind, brave dragon?" she asked.

"*GRRRgrrrgrr!*" Crackle exclaimed enthusiastically.

"Fly to the top of the highest tower," Aurora instructed. "Then blow the largest, brightest flames you can to help guide my parents to the castle."

A moment later, the little dragon soared upwards.

"Be careful!" the princess called.

Everyone tried to see Crackle, but it was too dark.

Suddenly, gold and red flames lit up the sky above the watchtower. Crackle had done it!

Again and again, Crackle blew his flames.

At last, Phillip shouted, "I see King Stefan's coach! They're almost here!"

Everyone hurried to greet the visitors.

"The tower light saved us!" King Stefan exclaimed. "I need one like it!"

At that moment Crackle flew into the hall.

"Well, there he is! Our new tower light," King Hubert said with a laugh.

"A dragon?" King Stefan asked. "But dragons are danger–"

"Not Crackle," Aurora interrupted. "He's a brave and helpful dragon!"

# THE LITTLE MERMAID

## Ariel to the Rescue

"Oh, Eric! This is wonderful!" Ariel said excitedly as she twirled around the ballroom with her prince. "I can dance with you and see the ocean!"

"Do you miss your sea friends?" he asked.

"Sometimes," Ariel replied a bit sadly. "But I love being with you."

Bright and early the next morning, Prince Eric saw Ariel walking along the beach. He caught up with her, and they strolled together along the sand. The prince knew Ariel was hoping to visit Flounder and Sebastian, as well as her other friends from the sea. But they were nowhere to be found.

Eric and Ariel watched the waves crash on to the shore.

"It's rough out there today. If I were a fish, I think I might be too scared to come close to the shore," the prince said gently. "Don't worry, Ariel. We'll figure out a way to bring together the land and the sea."

At dusk, Ariel went to Eric.
"I was thinking about what you said
earlier," she said. "I want to show you
something."

Ariel led the prince to the quiet lagoon
they had rowed in long ago.

"Do you think my friends would feel safer
visiting me here?" she asked.

Eric rubbed his chin. "*Hmmm.* Maybe."

He had an idea, but he wanted to make sure it
would work before he said anything to Ariel.

But the princess wouldn't give up. Soon she had coaxed the baby to swim over to her.

"I wish there was something more we could do," Ariel said.

"I bet his mother is on the other side of that wall. Don't worry," Flounder said. "We'll find her!"

But a few days later, Sebastian and Flounder still hadn't found her.

"This is terrible," Sebastian said. "We have looked everywhere under the sea, but cannot find the baby's mother. What should we do?"

Ariel looked at the little dolphin. Tomorrow she would ask more of her friends from under the sea to help.

Later that night, Ariel awoke to the sound of thunder. From the palace, she saw big waves crashing on the shore.

Eric joined her. "Are you worried about that baby dolphin?" he asked.

"He must be terrified," Ariel replied. "We need to go to him."

Eric followed Ariel into the stormy night. When they arrived at the lagoon, Flounder was trying to calm the frightened baby dolphin.

Ariel climbed on to the lagoon wall and called to the sea creatures. "Help me, please! I am Ariel, princess of the seas. I need my father, King Triton."

A whale was the first to respond. Then a school of fish flashed their fins.

"Thank you!" the princess shouted.

Below the surface, sea creatures raced to find King Triton.

Ariel returned to Eric. "I know my father will be able to help," she told him.

While they waited, Eric jumped into the sea and led the dolphin to calmer waters.

Suddenly, there was a flash of light! King Triton had arrived. The storm quietened down. The baby dolphin's mother was at the lagoon gate, frantically trying to get in.

"Oh, dear!" Ariel exclaimed. "The gate won't open! She can't get in!"

Eric looked at King Triton. "Do you mind?"

"Not at all," the king replied. "Swim back, everyone!" He raised his trident and blasted down the wall.

The dolphins swam to each other, then the baby went to Triton to thank him.

That night, the moon rose. But there was no royal ball at the palace. Instead, Eric and Ariel returned to the lagoon to be with their friends.

The baby dolphin and his mother swam up and playfully splashed the prince and princess.

"I think that means we are forgiven!" Ariel said with a laugh.